Loud Sounds, Quiet Sounds

Julia Bellish

Rosen
REAL
READERS

Rosen Classroom Books and Materials
New York

1

A train is loud.

A deer is quiet.

A bell is loud.

A bee is quiet.

A baby can be loud.

A baby can be quiet.

Words to Know

baby

bee

bell

deer

train